All Aboard!

Corinne Albaut - Grégoire Mabire

ZERO TO TEN

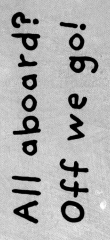

All aboard? Off we go!

Goodbye, grey city!

faster than all the cars.

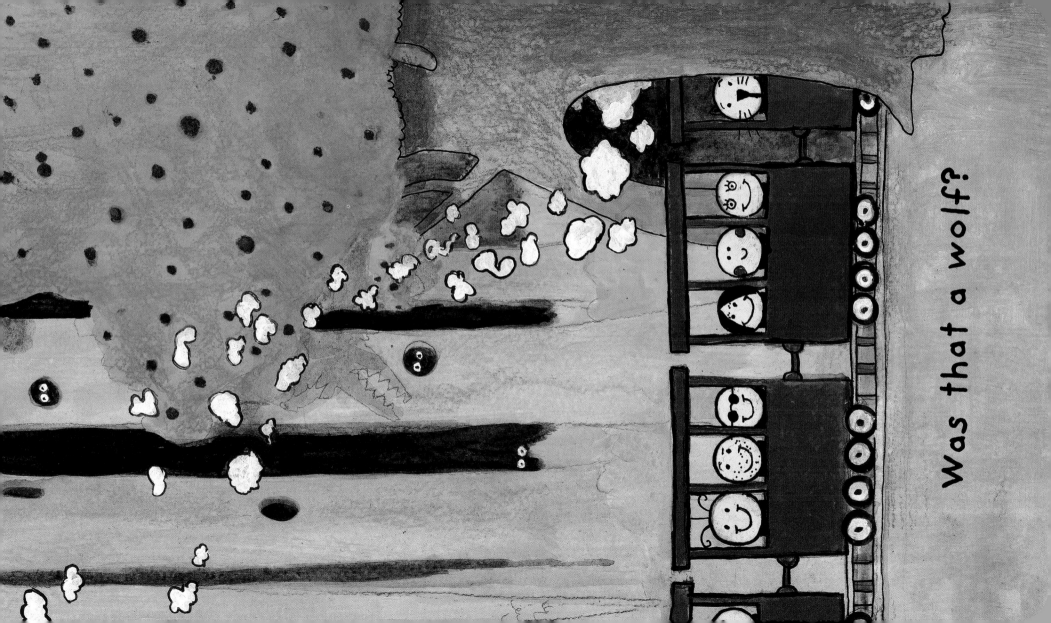

Was that a wolf?

Is that the sea already?

Oh no,
just a river.

Look – a field of cotton wool!

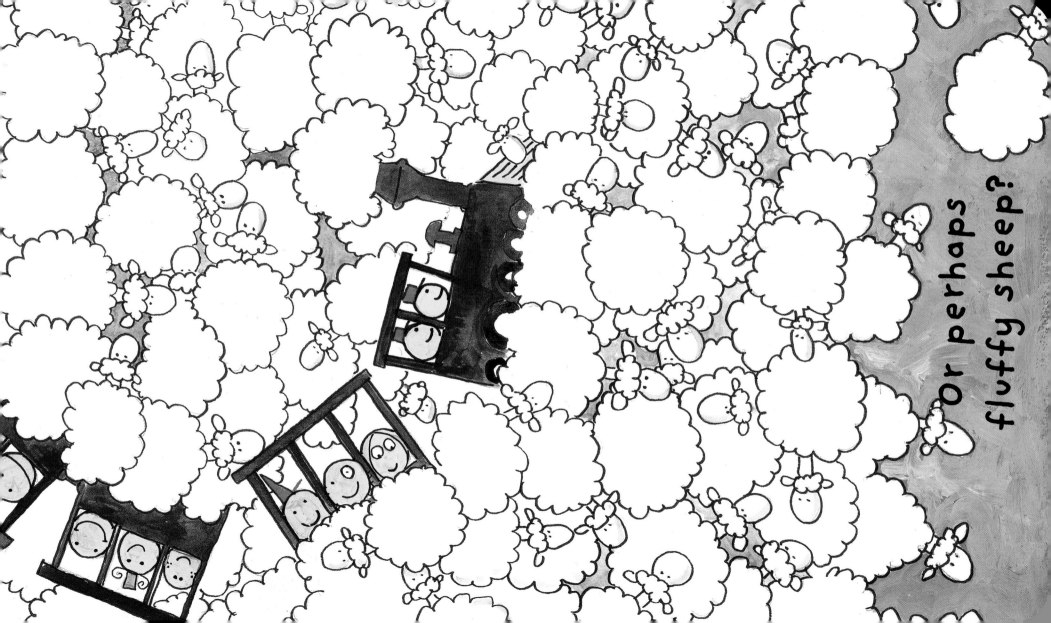

Or perhaps fluffy sheep?

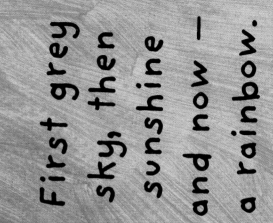

First grey
sky, then
sunshine
and now —
a rainbow.

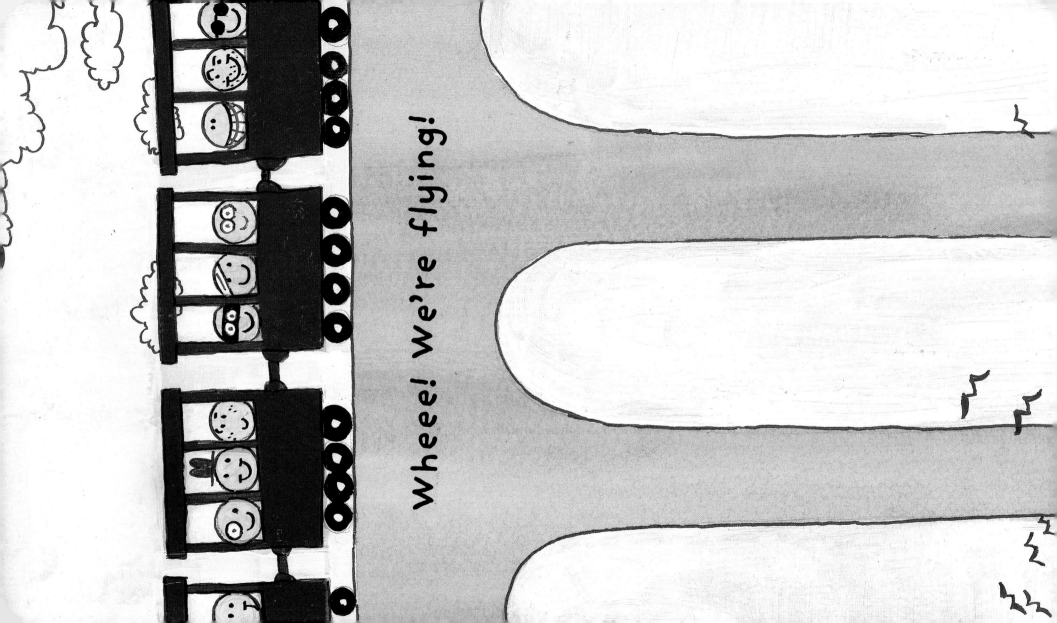

Wheee! We're flying!

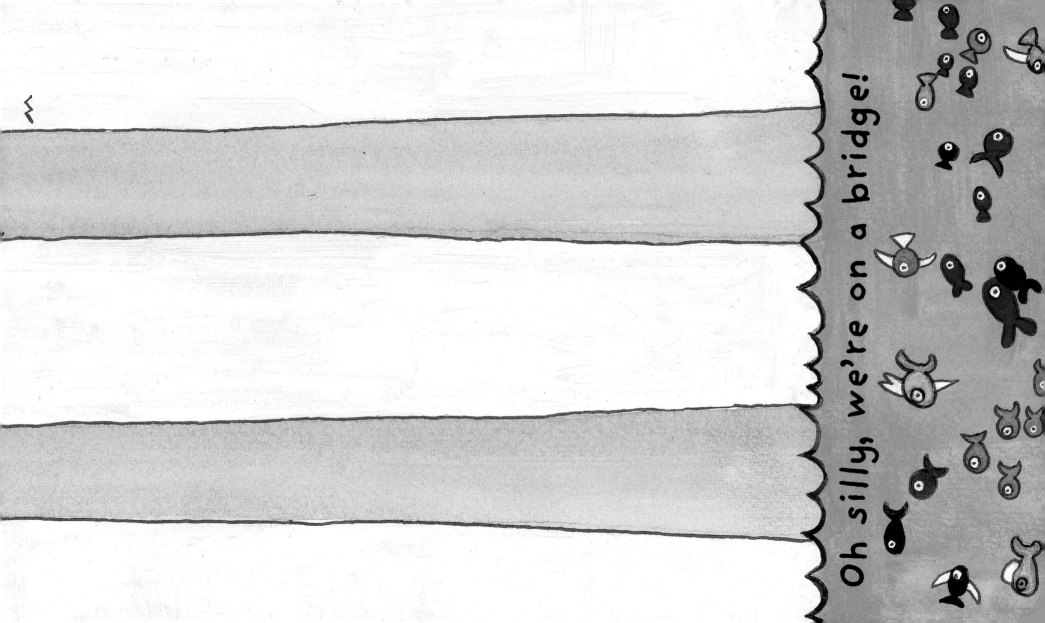

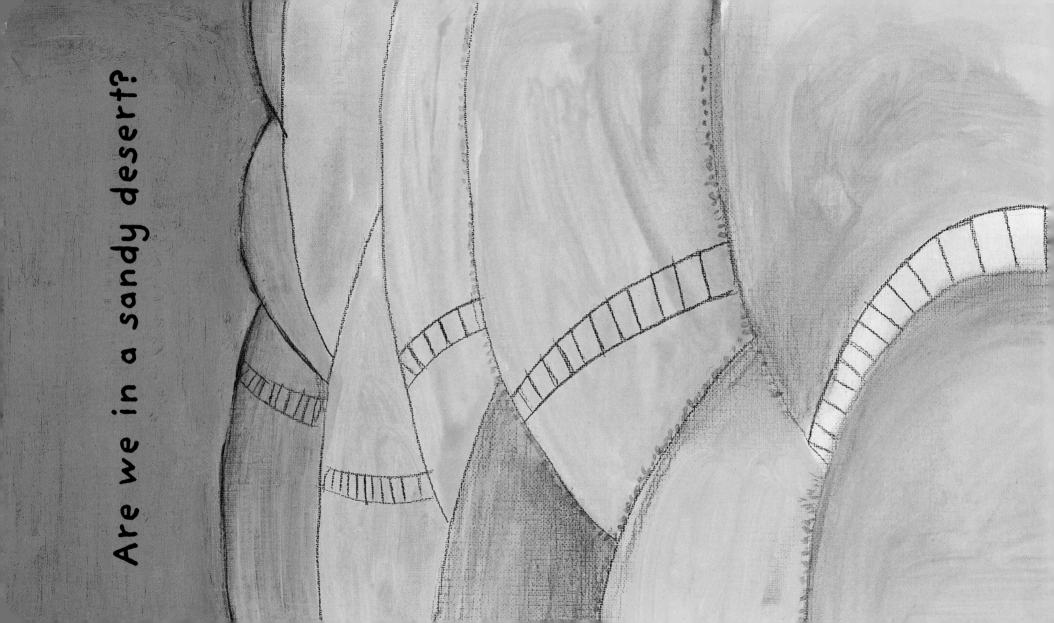

Are we in a sandy desert?

A train going the other way. They're coming back from their holidays.

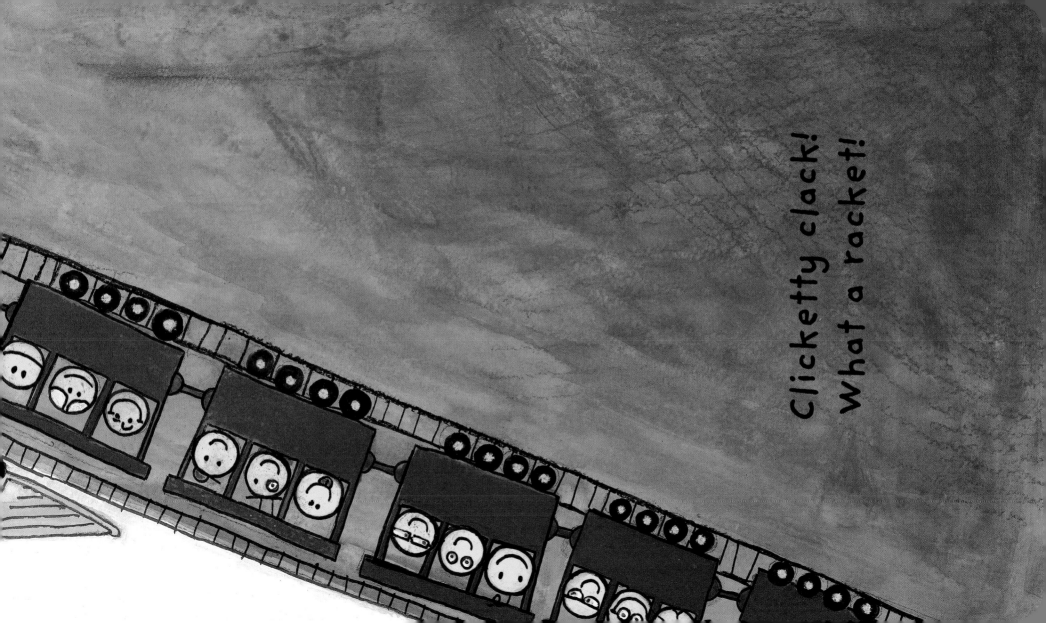

Clicketty clack!
What a racket!

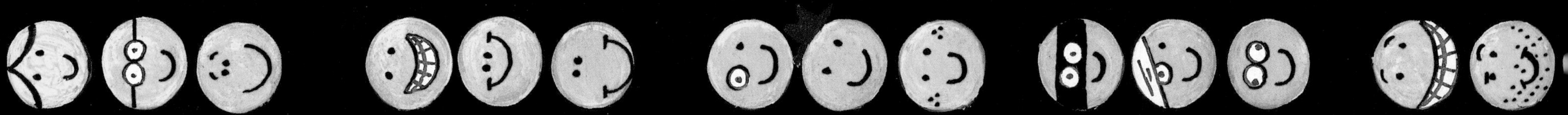

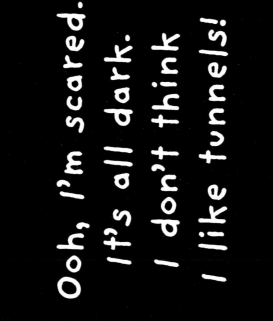

Ooh, I'm scared.
It's all dark.
I don't think
I like tunnels!

Hurrah, we're slowing down —
here's the station.